P9-DCW-929

Mr. Putter & Tabby
Catch the Cold

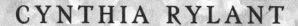

CYNTHIA RYLANT

Mr. Putter & Tabby
Catch the Cold

Illustrated by

ARTHUR HOWARD

Harcourt, Inc.
San Diego   New York   London

For Eustathia, who makes people better
—C. R.

For Joan, Sarah, Uncle Jeremy, and Joey
—A. H.

Text copyright © 2002 by Cynthia Rylant
Illustrations copyright © 2002 by Arthur Howard

www.HarcourtBooks.com

Library of Congress Cataloging-in-Publication Data
Rylant, Cynthia.
Mr. Putter & Tabby catch the cold/Cynthia Rylant;
illustrated by Arthur Howard.
p.   cm.
Summary: When Mr. Putter catches a cold, his friend Mrs. Teaberry
sends over some special treats to help him feel better.
[1. Cold (Disease)—Fiction. 2. Sick—Fiction.]
I. Howard, Arthur, ill. II. Title.
PZ7.R982Msc 2002
[E]—dc21   2001002949
ISBN 0-15-202414-X

Manufactured in China

First edition
A C E G H F D B

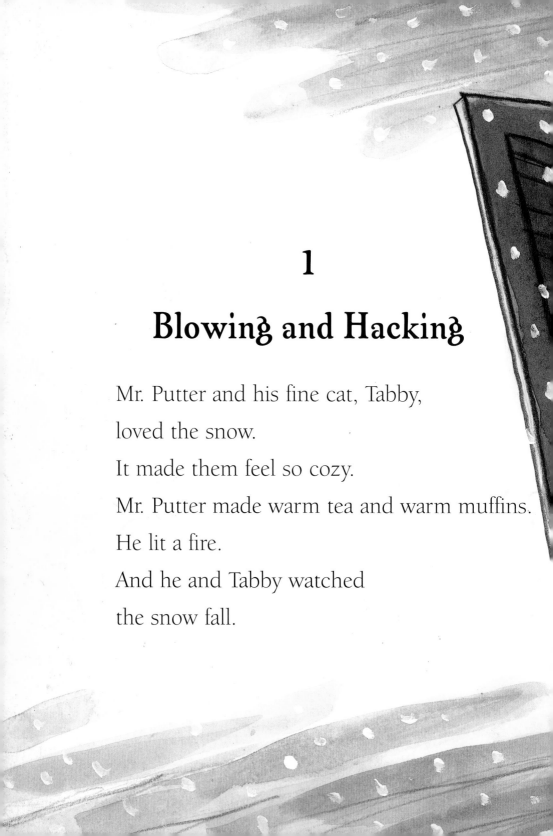

1

Blowing and Hacking

Mr. Putter and his fine cat, Tabby,
loved the snow.
It made them feel so cozy.
Mr. Putter made warm tea and warm muffins.
He lit a fire.
And he and Tabby watched
the snow fall.

One day Mr. Putter went out in
the snow without his hat.
He wanted to read the funnies in the
newspaper so much that he forgot it.

When he came back in, he said to Tabby,
"Tabby, I forgot my hat. I hope
I don't catch a cold."

Tabby sat on Mr. Putter's head to keep it
warm while he read the funnies.
She tried to help him not catch a cold.
She did her best.

But Mr. Putter caught one, anyway.
The next day he was sneezing and coughing
and blowing and hacking.
He felt miserable.

"Colds aren't so much fun when
you're old," he said to Tabby.

When Mr. Putter was a boy, he had almost *liked* colds.

He always got spoiled.

His mother brought him warm soup
and minty tea
and adventure books.

Mr. Putter *loved* adventure books.

But now he was old.

He was old with a cold.

And he had no one to spoil him.

2

Mrs. Teaberry

Mr. Putter's phone rang.

He picked it up and said, *"Ah-choo!"*

"Mr. Putter?" someone said.

It was Mrs. Teaberry, Mr. Putter's
good friend and neighbor.
"I caught a cold," said Mr. Putter.
"Oh my goodness!" said Mrs. Teaberry.
"I'll be right over!"

"Oh no," said Mr. Putter.
"You shouldn't come over, Mrs. Teaberry.
You might catch my cold. And it's not
good to be old with a cold."
Tabby rubbed against Mr. Putter
to help him feel better.

"Ah-choo!" went Mr. Putter

in Tabby's face.

She decided to stay on his lap.

"You need someone to look after
you," said Mrs. Teaberry.
"I'll be fine," said Mr. Putter.
"You need someone," said Mrs. Teaberry.
"I'll be fine," said Mr. Putter.
"You *really* need someone,"
said Mrs. Teaberry.
"I'll *really* be fine,"
said Mr. Putter.

"I'll send Zeke," said Mrs. Teaberry.

"What?" said Mr. Putter.

3

Zeke

Twenty minutes later there was
a scratching at the door.
It was Mrs. Teaberry's good dog, Zeke.
He had a Thermos strapped to his back
and he was wagging his tail.

"Thank you, Zeke!" said Mr. Putter,
patting Zeke's head.
Zeke wagged and went home.

Mr. Putter and Tabby looked inside
the Thermos.
"Chicken soup!" said Mr. Putter.
"Hooray!"
Tabby purred.
She loved chicken soup.

Mr. Putter and Tabby were having
their soup when there was
another scratching at the door.

It was Zeke again.

He had another Thermos strapped
to his back.

"Thank you, Zeke!" said Mr. Putter.

Zeke wagged and went home.

Mr. Putter and Tabby looked inside
the Thermos.
"Peppermint tea with honey sticks!"
said Mr. Putter. "Yippee!"

Tabby purred.

She loved honey sticks.

Mr. Putter and Tabby ate their soup
and drank their tea.

Mr. Putter was feeling much better.
But he wished he had one more thing.
He felt so selfish.
But he couldn't help it.
He phoned Mrs. Teaberry.

"Mrs. Teaberry, the soup and the
tea are wonderful," he said.
"Wonderful!" said Mrs. Teaberry.
"But...," said Mr. Putter.
"But?" asked Mrs. Teaberry.

"Would you perhaps have…?" said Mr. Putter.

"Would I perhaps have…?" said Mrs. Teaberry.

"An adventure book?" asked Mr. Putter.

"*Of course!*" said Mrs. Teaberry.

"You do?" asked Mr. Putter.

"Yes, I do," said Mrs. Teaberry. "But the book really belongs to Zeke."

"Zeke?" asked Mr. Putter.

"It's about a brave dog," said Mrs. Teaberry. "It's Zeke's favorite."

"Ummm," said Mr. Putter, "do you think
he would loan it to me?"

"Only if he gets to come along,"
said Mrs. Teaberry. "Zeke is very attached
to his book."

Mr. Putter thought about it.

The adventure book came with Zeke attached.

Could he manage Zeke *and* a cold?

Would Zeke be good?

Or would he be...Zeke?

Mr. Putter was desperate.

"Of course Zeke may come with his book,"
said Mr. Putter.
"Wonderful!" said Mrs. Teaberry.

A few minutes later there was a scratching at the door.

4

The Best Cold

It was surprising.

It was amazing.

Zeke was good!

Zeke was fine!

Zeke was *perfect*!

(As long as you were reading his

adventure book to him.)

Mr. Putter and Tabby and Zeke

curled up in Mr. Putter's bed

and read all day long.

Mr. Putter sounded a little funny
with his stuffy nose.
But Zeke and Tabby didn't mind.
They wanted to hear about
the brave dog.

Mr. Putter read and read
while Tabby purred
and Zeke wagged.

And when the brave dog's story was over,
they all snuggled up and went to sleep—
full of soup and tea and adventure.
It was the best cold Mr. Putter
ever caught.

The illustrations in this book were done in pencil, watercolor,
gouache, and Sennelier pastels on 250-gram cotton rag paper.
The display type was set in Artcraft.
The text type was set in Berkeley Old Style Book.
Color separations by Colourscan Co. Pte. Ltd., Singapore
Manufactured by South China Printing Company, Ltd., China
This book was printed on totally chlorine-free Nymolla Matte Art paper.
Production supervision by Sandra Grebenar and Pascha Gerlinger
Designed by Arthur Howard and Carolyn Stafford